Data Viz!

D1572791

The world is one
large database,

full of information
all over the place.

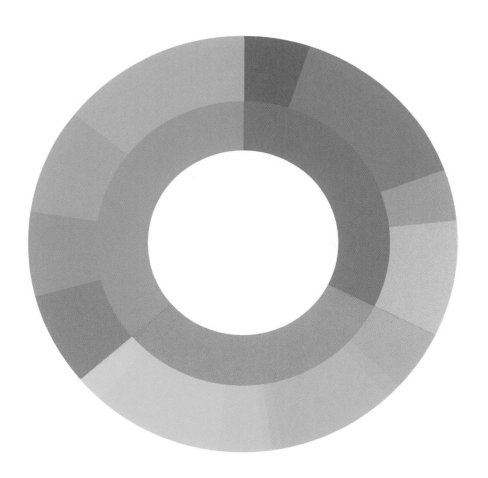

Some is messy and some is clean,

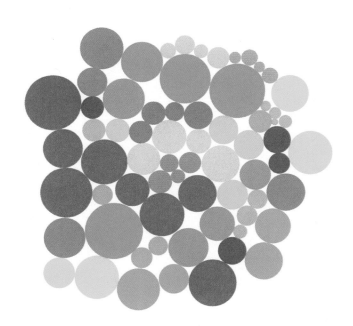

all too often, leaving
the story unseen.

That's when data viz comes to play,

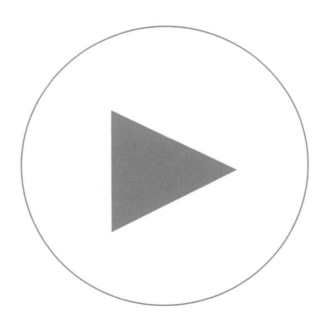

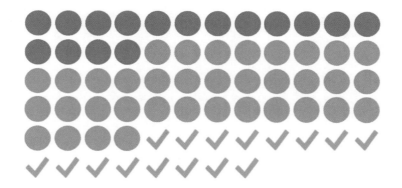

**to give the data
it's fair say!**

Data viz comes in all colors, shapes, and sizes.

Blending for insights and sometimes surprises!

Most common of all is graphing a line,

showing movements and trends over time.

A bar chart can be vertical or be flat,

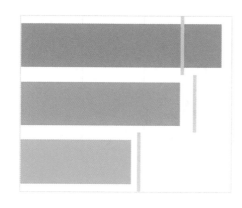

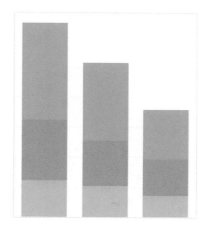

**show progress toward
a target or be stacked.**

A pie chart shows proportion on a plot,

some folks love them, while others do not.

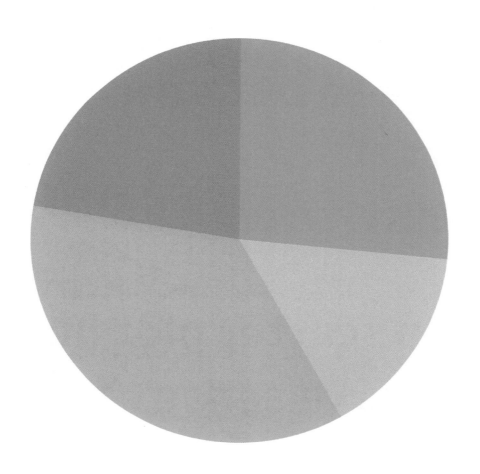

If there's many points to put on a chart,

a scatter plot helps make sense of all parts.

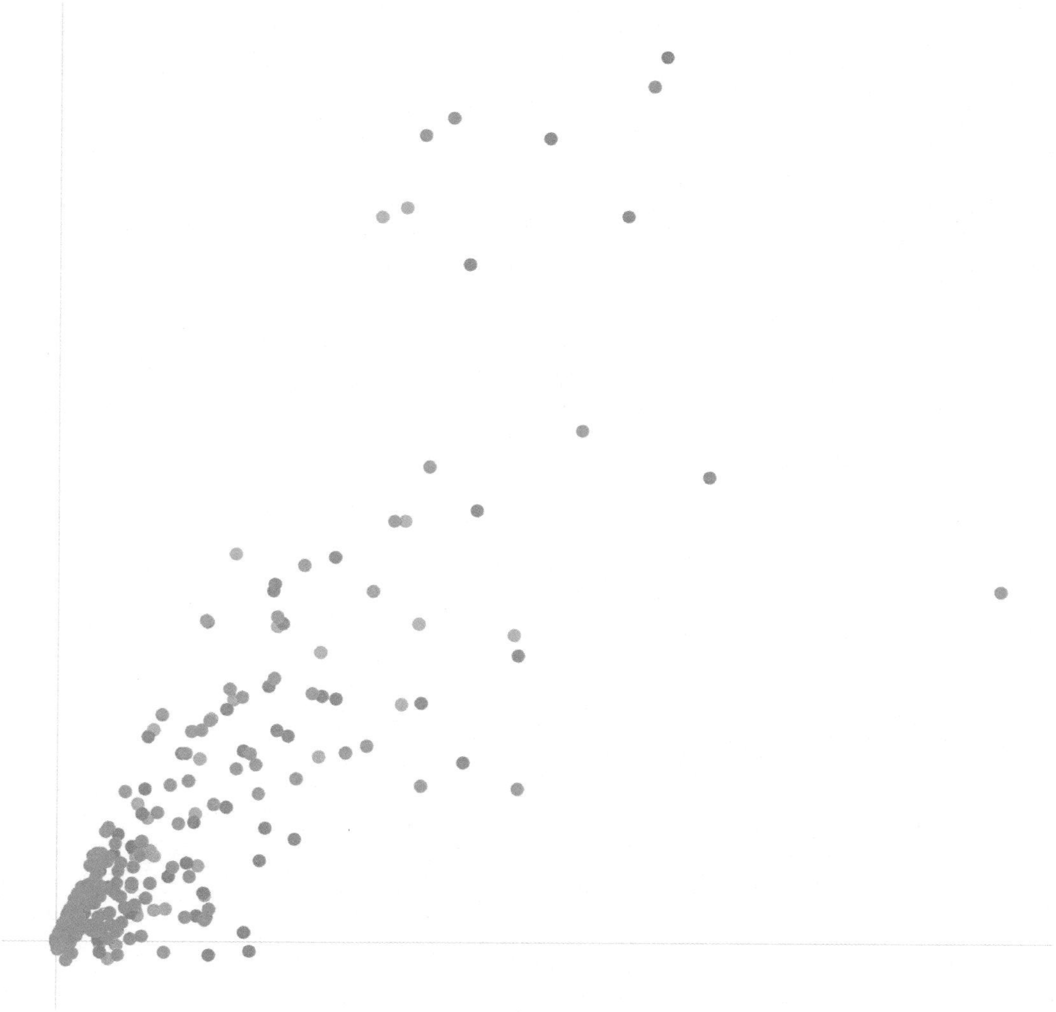

Box and whisker plots show the extremes,

as well as all values in between.

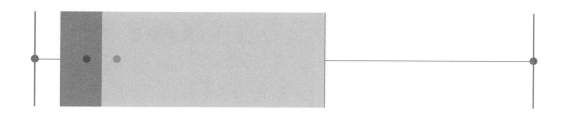

With the data now charted and the answer moved toward,

it's time to create a colorful dashboard!

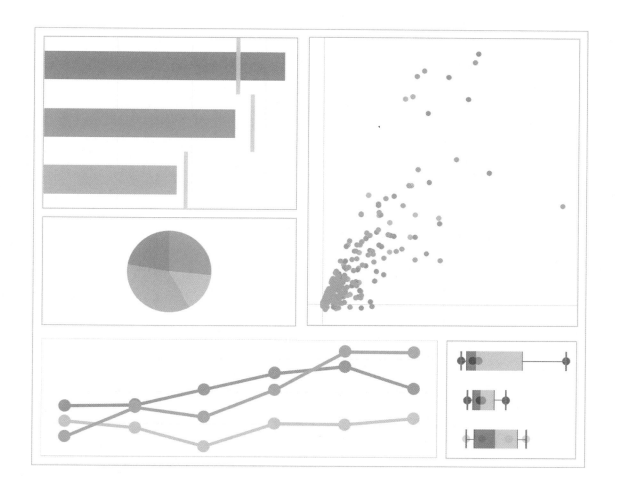

The End!

For my son Jameson,

Your creativity and curiosity motivate me to
dream and dare more than I ever would.

Made in the USA
Middletown, DE
18 May 2022

65915262R00015